C115

01. AUG 01

28. NOV 08

05. NOV 09.

27 SEP 2011

- 8 AUG 2013

15 AUG 2013

- 6 AUG 2015

KU-525-534

CORNHILL LIBRARY
Tel: 696209

PLEASE RETURN TO THE ABOVE LIBRARY OR ANY OTHER ABERDEEN CITY LIBRARY, ON OR BEFORE THE DUE DATE. TO RENEW, PLEASE QUOTE THE DUE DATE AND THE BARCODE NUMBER.

Aberdeen City Council
Library & Information Services

You do not need to read this page - just get on with the book!

First published 1999 in Great Britain by
Barrington Stoke Ltd
10 Belford Terrace, Edinburgh, EH4 3DQ
Reprinted 1999 (twice)

This edition published 2001

Copyright © 1999, 2001 Hazel Townson
Illustrations © Philippe Dupasquier
The moral right of the author has been asserted in accordance with
the Copyright, Designs and Patents Act 1988
ISBN 1-902260-86-4
Previously published by Barrington Stoke Ltd under ISBN 1-902260-11-2

Printed by Polestar AUP Aberdeen Ltd
1902 260 864 5280

Meet The Author - Hazel Townson

What is your favourite animal?
A dog
What is your favourite boy's name?
Christopher
What is your favourite girl's name?
Catherine
What is your favourite food?
Strawberries
What is your favourite music?
Classical, especially Mahler
What is your favourite hobby?
Table tennis

Meet The Illustrator - Philippe Dupasquier

What is your favourite animal?
A tiger
What is your favourite boy's name?
Jonathan
What is your favourite girl's name?
Sophie
What is your favourite food?
Oysters
What is your favourite music?
Rock music
What is your favourite hobby?
Drawing

For Sue Stephenson, a great champion of children's books

Contents

Chapter 1
A Terrible Mistake

Ronnie Batwell hated all sport. It was kids' stuff. He knew he could kick, catch, run or jump better than anyone else, but he didn't see why he should bother. It was all too much like hard work, for one thing. Let the others sweat and strain and limp home covered in mud. He would rather watch the telly any day.

If anyone had called him lazy he would simply have grinned and shrugged his shoulders. Let them think what they liked.

Ronnie knew he wasn't lazy, just sensible. After all, he was the one with no bruises, no blistered feet, no aches and pains.

Tuesdays and Fridays were Ronnie's difficult days, for there was sport all afternoon. But he usually managed a pretty good excuse, such as back trouble, a dental appointment or a sudden attack of hay fever.

But there was one thing Ronnie could not dodge, and that was Sports Day.

On Sports Day there was no escape for anyone. The headteacher, Mr Borden, was a great believer in Team Spirit. Every child must play some part, however small. There was always a relay race or a tug-of-war to cater for the 'duds' and that was usually where Ronnie ended up because he'd skipped the other heats.

Not this year, though!

Ronnie scanned the lists on the notice board and was amazed to find himself with nothing to do. His name had not been added to a single list.

A new sports teacher called Springer had only just come to school and was still learning his way around. Sports Day loomed ahead before he had even met all the staff. He had to draw up the lists in such a hurry that Ronnie Batwell's name was left out.

Ronnie could hardly believe his luck. He knew he should point out the mistake, but he wasn't going to. He reckoned it would be easy enough to get away with it. He would simply flop about on the field in his PE outfit, looking as though he had just taken part in something. Everyone would be far too busy to guess the truth. Especially Mr Borden, who had been struggling hard to pay all the school bills and had not been able to keep his usual eye on things. People had even been saying that the Head would miss Sports Day altogether.

Ah, but it is never wise to rely on rumours! Mr Borden was a man who missed nothing. He knew the names of all his pupils and every move they made. Three days before Sports Day he looked over the programme with Mr Springer and at once discovered that Ronnie's name was missing.

"Didn't young Ronnie come and tell you that he wasn't on any list?" the headmaster demanded grimly. "He knows quite well that nobody misses out on Sports Day. Nobody!"

"Er – he hasn't said anything to me yet, headmaster!"

Mr Borden frowned.

"Well, he's had plenty of time to do so. He's trying to wriggle out of it, you mark my words."

Mr Borden took a deep breath. Then he said, "Right! That lad is for the high jump."

What the headmaster meant, of course, was that our hero was in real trouble. But Mr Springer, not yet used to the ways of his new boss, took this at its face value and put Ronnie's name down on the high jump list. He might as well have condemned the lad to death.

Chapter 2
One Jump Ahead

When Mr Springer told Ronnie of his fate, the poor lad could not hide his shock.

"But sir, I can't jump!" he protested. "I've got this funny heel."

Mr Springer stared at Ronnie's feet.

"You look perfectly fit to me. Have you ever tried to jump?" he asked reasonably.

"Well, no, sir. But I'm sure I'd be no good. I just haven't got it in me, sir."

"No need to be modest, Ronnie. If your headmaster thinks you can do it, then at least you have to try," Springer insisted. "Meet me on the field at half-past eight tomorrow morning, then again after school, and we'll put you through your paces."

Ronnie scowled. The high jump was no joke. In fact, it was jolly hard work and involved a lot of boring training.

"Honest, I can't do it anyway, sir, because I just can't make it to school for half-past eight. The bus doesn't get here until ten to nine."

"Then you'll either have to walk or catch an earlier bus for once, won't you?"

"Sir, Mum won't let me walk in case I get run over. And she won't let me stay late after school because the bus gets full in the rush hour," babbled Ronnie.

Mr Springer sighed. Ronnie could see he was rapidly losing patience.

"Oh, come on now! Your mother will be proud that you are in the team. And YOU should be proud that Mr Borden has such faith in you. You don't want to let everyone down, do you? So just make an effort and be there tomorrow. That's an order."

"Yes, sir!"

Ronnie looked so miserable that Mr Springer added more kindly, "You don't know what you can do until you try, and I'll be there to help you. All you need is a bit of practice and plenty of confidence."

The only thing Ronnie felt confident about was that this was the worst day of his life. He'd

been caught out at last. The poor lad reached home in a state of black depression. His classmates would think it the best joke ever. He could already see them collapsing with laughter all over the sports field. Even worse, if his parents found out he was in something as important as the high jump final they would want to come and watch. That might lead to all sorts of complications.

Ronnie's parents were still at work. Ronnie let himself in to the empty house with the key he kept on a string round his neck. Then he sat brooding on the stairs. How could he wriggle out of this nightmare? The thought of all that exertion was making him feel really ill.

Ill?

Suddenly he had a brainwave. Why, that was it! The solution was simple. He would stay off school tomorrow, pretending to be sick. And the next day. And the day after that, the Dreaded Day

itself. He could easily forge his Mum's handwriting on a note.

The relief was wonderful. Why hadn't he thought of it sooner? He had never bunked off school before. Still, most of his classmates managed the odd day or two without being caught, so why shouldn't he?

Feeling much brighter, he began to make plans. He would set out for school as usual, but miss the bus. He had better not hang about the streets though. His Dad drove a delivery van and might zoom past at any moment. Instead, Ronnie would sneak back home after his folks had left for work. He could then get on with his Save the Earth project, so there would be no need even to feel guilty.

I've cracked it, thought Ronnie with glee.

Little did he know how wrong he was.

Chapter 3
Enter – A Murderer!

Next morning Ronnie got ready for school at his usual time. Nobody suspected a thing.

"Watch out for the traffic, love!" came his mother's daily warning as she hurried off to work.

"Come on, son, I'll give you a lift," joked Ronnie's Dad as he started up the delivery van.

He knew very well that Ronnie would rather die than be seen going to school with his Dad.

Ronnie waved goodbye and trotted off towards the bus stop. Then he hid in a shop doorway and kept watch. Once he knew the coast was clear he ran quickly back home and let himself in. He was certain he hadn't been spotted. Even the nosy couple next door had left for work.

He decided to hide in his bedroom in case anyone looked in through the downstairs windows. He had a desk up there, but soon grew sick of working on his project. Let the Earth save itself. For the moment Ronnie had other things on his mind.

One was the sick note. After many attempts, he saw that he could not make his handwriting look like his Mum's. The teacher would see that Ronnie had written it himself. Countless screwed-up sheets of paper landed in the waste bin. Then he took them out again in a panic. His Mum might decide to read them. He tore every sheet into tiny shreds.

All he could do now was to snaffle his Mum's next shopping-list. With that as a handwriting sample he could practise until he got it right.

After that, the morning stretched ahead like a year of boring Sundays. Was his watch slowing down? Maybe it needed a new battery. At last he decided to creep downstairs and risk making a sandwich.

The first thing he saw on the kitchen table was his Dad's newspaper. A bold, black headline on the front page said, BURGLAR KIDNAPS BOY. That caught Ronnie's imagination. He snatched up the paper at once and began to read.

The boy in the story was called Sam. He wasn't some distant stranger either. He lived in the very next town, only five miles away. That made the story even more interesting.

It seemed that while Sam's parents were out, Sam had come home to find a burglar robbing the house. The burglar had grabbed the boy and driven him off in a green Land Rover. Sam had not been seen since. There was a full-scale search going on. The police were even dragging a river and a lake. It was feared by now that the boy would not be found alive.

So that burglar was probably a murderer as well! Only five miles away, too. Had he been caught? Ronnie was anxious to read on and find out, but there was a sudden din outside the front door. A shuffling and thumping noise made him put down the newspaper and listen. It was much too late for the postman, so what could it be?

Ronnie waited uneasily for a knock or a ring at the doorbell. With luck it would only be someone he could ignore, such as a double-glazing salesman or the Daz doorstep challenge test. Unless – horror of horrors – it was somebody from school!

It turned out to be even worse than that. Ronnie could now hear a key scraping in the lock. Someone was actually opening the door! Just to prove it, a great draught of air blew up the hall.

Ronnie panicked. One of his parents must be coming home. Well, they had better not find him here. Quick as a blink, he slipped into the cubby-hole under the stairs where the boots and umbrellas were kept.

For a while he simply stood in the dark among the boots and listened. Somebody with heavy feet was tramping up and down the hall, making a lot of noise. It didn't sound like his Mum or Dad. In the end he grew curious. He opened the cubby-hole door a crack and peered out.

He was just in time to see a man making off up the hall with the television set. It certainly wasn't his Dad. Through the open front door Ronnie also saw a green Land Rover parked right outside the house.

A green Land Rover!

Ronnie remembered every detail of the newspaper article he had just read. Hairs rose on the back of his neck. This man in the hall, this thief making off with their telly, was probably

the same burglar who had kidnapped Sam. What was to stop him kidnapping Ronnie too, if he caught sight of him?

I could end up in the river – murdered! thought Ronnie.

He felt sick and dizzy. He swayed, lost his balance and fell against the cubby-hole door. The door swung open and crashed against the wall. The startled burglar turned – and the two of them came face to face.

The prospect of facing the high jump was nothing compared to this. Ronnie thought he would remember this moment for the rest of his life ... if he still had a life.

The burglar was not wearing a mask, as burglars are supposed to do. Ronnie found this even more frightening. It meant the man was sure he would get away with it. Anyone spotting him would think he was taking the telly away

for repair. It would never occur to them to raise the alarm or rush to the rescue of a boy who was about to be murdered.

The burglar now knew that Ronnie had seen his face.

He knows I'll remember it, too, Ronnie thought. How could I ever forget it? So that makes me his number one enemy. He'll have to murder me to shut me up, just as he did with Sam, only five miles from here.

Terrified, Ronnie crashed from his hiding place, leapt for the back door and fled.

Chapter 4
No Hiding Place

Ronnie was sure he would be followed.

True, the burglar had had his arms full but he would soon get rid of the telly. Then he could give chase in that wicked green Land Rover. Better keep off the roads, then. Ronnie dived down an alley and through the underpass which led into the park.

So far, so good, but he couldn't stay in the park all day. Nor was he keen to go and tell his

parents or the police. If he did, they'd find out that he hadn't been to school. Surely there must be somewhere safe to hide until the end of the school day? Then he could go home late, making sure he arrived after his Mum. Let her discover the burglary.

By that time, thought Ronnie, the burglar will know that I've not told on him. So perhaps he won't need to murder me after all.

But where was there a hiding place? It would have to be somewhere good, for this was a matter of life and death.

Suddenly Ronnie remembered something he had learnt at school. Churches gave sanctuary. If you hid in a church, nobody could touch you. Fired with new hope, he ran over to St. Steven's but the church door was locked. Yesterday someone had been in and painted rude words on the ends of the pews so the vicar was not taking any more chances.

Just my rotten luck! thought Ronnie.

He turned away, then saw the library close by the church. He would try that instead. After all, murder was pretty unlikely to happen in a library.

The children's library was always busy when Ronnie went there after school, but at this quiet time of day he found it almost deserted. Only three people were there – a woman with a toddler choosing picture books and the librarian, Mrs Oates. No hope of losing himself in a crowd, then. In fact, Ronnie could see that Mrs Oates already had her eye on him. He fled to the back of the room, grabbed the first book he saw and pretended to be studying it. All the same, that did not stop Mrs Oates from coming over to talk to him.

"Shouldn't you be in school?" she enquired pleasantly enough.

"I'm – er – doing a project on Save The Earth," Ronnie told her, which was the truth after all.

Mrs Oates peered over his shoulder.

"Well, you won't find much material for that in a book about ballet dancing."

Ronnie blushed and said nothing. Despite his famous imagination he was hopeless at lying.

"Has your teacher sent you here?" asked Mrs Oates.

"We – er – have to use our own inush – inash – initiative," stammered Ronnie, avoiding a direct answer.

He could see it had been a mistake to come in here. Pushing the book back into the wrong slot on the shelf, he mumbled something about forgetting his ticket, and hurried away.

For one reckless moment Ronnie had considered telling Mrs Oates that he was about to be murdered, yet he had decided she wouldn't believe him. She would probably ring up the school, or his Dad.

The trouble was, now that he had to leave the library where else could he go? To make matters worse, it was now raining hard. Curse the wretched Sports Day! Curse Springer and Borden! This was all their fault.

Chapter 5
One Shock After Another!

The rain was absolutely sheeting down by now and Ronnie was desperate to get under cover.

Well, there was always the Bymore shopping centre. In happier times this was one of Ronnie's favourite places. He loved hunting around for dropped coins. (He had once found a total of seventeen pence in a single day in there.)

Unfortunately it was quite a distance to the Bymore, which lay in the same direction as school. Ronnie was terrified of being spotted. He dodged from one shop doorway to another, like a clumsy spy on his first mission. Yet although he kept looking back, he saw no sign of a green Land Rover. By the time he arrived at the shopping centre he was pretty certain he had shaken off his pursuer.

What a relief!

He was so wet, though, that he had to prop himself against a radiator in Treater's toy shop to dry himself out. He still felt shaky, but much more hopeful. No Land Rover could possibly drive in here. As his clothes dried off so he slowly calmed down. He even began to think of himself as a bit of a hero. After all, he had dodged a murderer and cheated Death.

"Life isn't over yet," Ronnie told himself.

Gradually he began to take an interest in where he was. And there, right in front of him, he spotted a model bus of a type he had never seen before. It must be a new make.

Ronnie was keen to take a closer look because he collected model buses. He moved over to the stall and picked up the bus. He was just studying the price and wondering how long it would take him to save up for it, when a hand fell on to his shoulder.

“Now then, laddie,” cried Mr Treater, the shop owner. “I’ve been watching you. Choosing your moment for a bit of shoplifting, eh? I’d stop playing truant and get back to school if I were you.”

What a shock! For one awful moment Ronnie thought the burglar had got him. But fancy being taken for a shoplifter! He had never in his life made off with anything that wasn’t his. Except for the lost coins he picked up, but those were finders-keepers.

"Honest, I was only looking ..." he began.

"That's what they all say. Got any money?"

"I've got my bus fare ..."

Ronnie almost added "... to school", but checked himself in time.

"Right, well you come back in the school holidays with your pocket money and you can have a good look then."

Mr Treater prised the bus from Ronnie's hand and steered the boy firmly towards the door. Ronnie hurried away, his head hung in shame. He'd never been so humiliated in his life.

"Here, look where you're going!" a woman shouted as he walked right into her.

“Kids!” cried her friend in disgust. “No manners at all! And anyway, shouldn’t he be in school?”

Ronnie started running again. One of these bossy folks might force him to go back to school. He would have gone on running, too, if

he hadn't suddenly spotted his Dad's television set.

A man was just placing it in the middle of a shop window. Ronnie stopped and stared. It was a second-hand shop. A sign above the window said, GET YOUR ALMOST-NEW TVs, VIDEOS AND RADIOS HERE. ALL TOP QUALITY GOODS.

Ronnie peered at the television set. There was no doubt about it being theirs. Ronnie recognised on its side a nasty 'L' shaped scratch he had made one Sunday afternoon when he'd missed the dartboard.

So the burglar had come into the shopping centre after all! Perhaps he was here at this very minute, waiting to pounce? Ronnie looked around in fresh terror. The place was packed with shoppers, and most of the men could well be the burglar. Although Ronnie had thought he would never forget that face, he was sure now that he could see it everywhere in dozens of different shapes and sizes.

Right, this was it! Now he would have to tell the police while the evidence was still there for them to see. If he waited, the telly might be sold.

He had passed a telephone box somewhere near Treater's shop. He could dial 999 for free. He spun round intending to run back to it – and came face to face with the burglar who was just leaving the second-hand shop.

Chapter 6
A Leap for Dear Life

Ronnie had never run so fast in his life. His reluctance to exert himself disappeared like ice in a microwave. He wove in and out of the crowds, dodging shopping-trolleys, prams and zimmer-frames with amazing skill. He flew along as if on roller-blades. It was surprising what you could do when your life was at stake.

From time to time he caught glimpses of his pursuer in various shop-windows. This made him run even faster. Before he knew it, he was outside the shopping centre again and hurtling down Hill Street towards school.

Towards school?

Well, he no longer cared about being caught for playing truant. School was suddenly a haven, the safest place to be. Even Mr Borden would not stand by and watch him being murdered. Ronnie couldn't get there fast enough.

Hill Street was pretty steep and the school was at the bottom, surrounded by playing-fields. The pavements were wet and slippery from the rain. Ronnie began to lose control. As he shot down the hill at amazing speed he began to realise that he would not be able to stop himself.

What could he do?

There was a high hedge all the way around the playing fields. There were two gates in the hedge, but these were on the opposite side,

in Brown Street. Ronnie found himself hurtling straight towards the hedge!

That hedge was about a metre and a half high – but suddenly Ronnie Batwell flung himself up into the air and flew right over it. He landed on the grass of the playing-field just as Mr Springer was chasing home the last dawdler from a sprint round the field.

Mr Springer was amazed.

"I know I told you to practise, Ronnie, but I didn't expect you to risk your neck by leaping over the hedge," he shouted.

Ronnie was too breathless to answer. He lay panting on the grass while Mr Springer hurried over to see if the boy was hurt. Once the teacher was sure there was no damage done, he helped Ronnie to his feet.

"Well, at least this gets rid of your objections," he told Ronnie. "Now you see that you can jump as well as anybody, and better than most. A pity you missed our early session, but I'll see you after school as arranged. And don't leap any more hedges in the meantime."

Mr Springer suddenly seemed like a knight in shining armour. He might have been the original cause of Ronnie's trouble, but if anybody was to save Ronnie now, it must be him. Ronnie took a deep breath and blurted out his story.

"Sir, there's a murderer after me! He's been chasing me all through the shopping centre. That's why I jumped the hedge."

The teacher tutted.

"Well, that's the most original excuse for a morning off that I've ever heard."

"Honest, sir, he burgled our house and I saw him, so he's following me. They think he's already murdered a boy called Sam."

"And I think you deliberately stayed away to miss the high jump practice, so you can save your imagination for the English lesson. And you'd better turn up after school, my lad. You've no excuse now. You're a natural."

"But sir ... !"

"Not another word, Ronnie. Get off to your classroom and just be thankful that I don't intend to repeat your ridiculous story to the headmaster."

Ronnie groaned.

Fate seemed determined to make a fool of him one way or another in this high jump business. Still, at least it was better than being murdered.

Chapter 7
A Big Surprise

Ronnie made his way across the playing field towards the door nearest his classroom. He wasn't exactly hurrying, as he still needed time to think up a good excuse.

Suddenly he spotted a van outside the gym door. It was his Dad's van! Mr Batwell was delivering new benches to the school.

Ronnie started running.

"Dad! Dad! Wait for me!" he yelled, as his father walked back to his van, ready to drive away.

Now at last there was someone who would believe Ronnie's story, even if it did land him in trouble.

"We've been burgled, Dad! And the burglar's trying to murder me!" blurted out Ronnie as Dad turned towards him in amazement.

"You what?"

"It's true, Dad!"

Mr Batwell could see that his son was most upset. He put an arm round the boy's shaking shoulders.

"All right, now just calm down and take it slowly, son. Who's been burgled? Your class?"

"No, we have! Us. Our family. Our house! This burglar's pinched our telly, and he has a green Land Rover so he's a murderer as well. It says so in your paper."

"Whoa! Steady on!"

Ronnie's Dad began to laugh.

"If you mean Jack Briggs, he's been swapping our old telly for a new one. It was supposed to be a surprise. Wait till you see it! Teletext, cable and the lot. You'll be over the moon. I gave Jack Briggs a key so he could sneak it in before any of you got home. It's part of my birthday present to your Mum."

A thought struck Dad.

"Just a minute, how did you know about it anyway?"

Here it comes, thought Ronnie. Still, he knew he would have to face up to everything in the end. Shamefaced, he made a full confession.

"But how was I supposed to know he wasn't a murderer? He was chasing me, Dad!"

"He probably saw how scared you were and wanted to explain who he was. Or else he thought YOU were a burglar, running off like that."

Ronnie struggled to take all this in. He felt angry now. Somebody – he wasn't quite sure who – had made a fool of him. The only good thing about it was that surely his Dad could see he was in no fit state to take part in Sports Day training. He would easily get Ronnie off the hook.

No such luck! Mr Springer came over just then to see why Ronnie hadn't gone back into school. So Dad had to explain who he was. He also repeated everything that Ronnie had just told him.

"It's all a silly misunderstanding, but you can see the boy's upset."

Mr Springer chose not to mention that if Ronnie had come to school in the first place, none of this would have happened. The teacher was too pleased at having discovered a possible new champion. So he did not complain but described how the boy had come bowling hot-foot down the hill like some junior Lynford Christie and best of all, how he had leapt clear over the hedge.

"It was one of the best jumps I've ever seen. And with a bit of practice he'll even improve on that."

Mr Batwell beamed with delight.

"I always knew he had it in him," he declared with pride. "Just wait till I tell his mother our lad's likely to win the high jump on Sports Day. Some birthday present that'll be!"

There was a shriek of dismay.

"But Dad, look at the state I'm in! You surely can't let me … " began Ronnie in utter desperation.

His Dad did not seem to hear. His mind was entirely taken up with the triumphs to come.

Suddenly inspired, he laid an encouraging hand on Mr Springer's shoulder.

"Tell you what! Since the lad ran down that hill so fast, why don't you put him in for the hundred metres as well?"

ABERDEEN
CITY
LIBRARIES

Who is Barrington Stoke?

Barrington Stoke was a famous and much-loved story-teller. He travelled from village to village carrying a lantern to light his way. He arrived as it grew dark and when the young boys and girls of the village saw the glow of his lantern, they hurried to the central meeting place. They were full of excitement and expectation, for his stories were always wonderful.

Then Barrington Stoke set down his lantern. In the flickering light the listeners were enthralled by his tales of adventure, horror and mystery. He knew exactly what they liked best and he loved telling a good story. And another. And then another. When the lantern burned low and dawn was nearly breaking, he slipped away. He was gone by morning, only to appear the next day in some other village to tell the next story.

If you loved this story, why don't you read . . .

The Secret Room

by Hazel Townson

How would you like to go back in time? Adam thinks the school stationery store may hold the clue to a secret room. But to his horror, he finds he has gone back in time - to the Second World War.

You can order this book directly from Macmillan Distribution Ltd, Brunel Road, Houndmills, Basingstoke, Hampshire RG21 6XS Tel: 01256 302699